SCARE-IFIC SECRETS

Written by the ghoulfriends of Monster High!

studio fun BOOKS

White Plains, New York • Montréal, Québec • Bath, United Kingdom

SIGN IN, GHOULFRIENDS!

Hey, ghouls. Frankie here! This is our brand-new freaky-fabulous passbook. I read all about it in Monster Beat magazine—we'll each write questions down, and all of us have to answer honestly. :) I think it'll be a scary-fun way to get to know each other even better!

NAME:
Draculaura
Daughter of Dracula
Vegetarian vampire,
soooo excited to share
my scare-ific secrets
with you ghouls!

NAME: Clawdeen
Daughter of the Werewolf
Resident fiercely
fashionable werewolf,
ready to show you
ghouls how it's done. ;)

NAME:

Frankie

Daughter of Frankenstein

I may not be the new ghoul anymore, but I still have a lot to learn about being a teen.

NAME: Cleo

Daughter of the Mummy
The most royally
important ghoul
you'll ever meet.

NAME:

Lagoona

Daughter of the Sea Monster
I'm an easygoing monster who
tends to go with the flow.

NAME:

Ghoulia

Daughter of the Zombies
Some monsters say I'm the
brainiest ghoul at school.

Ever since my first day at Monster High, I've been drawn to History class. I guess it's because I still have so much to learn about the world around me—plus it helps me understand my ghoulfriends and their freaky-fab scaritages!

—Frankie

Some vampires love to lurk and bite
Or hide in shadows all the night
But this vampire prefers to write
For poetry is her delight!

(Creative Writing...if it wasn't obvious ;)

—Draculaura

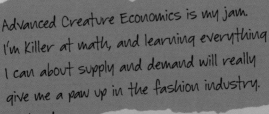

CLAWCULUS

GOOD NUMBER PUBLISHERS

Advanced Creature Economics is my jam. I'm Killer at math, and learning everything I can about supply and demand will really give me a paw up in the fashion industry.

—Clawdeen

You're so dead-icated to your dream, Clawdeen. It's way inspirational!

Drama. My ability to purrfectly mimic another monster's voice or accent makes this the purrfect class for me.
   —Toralei

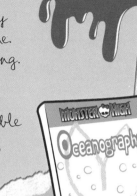

Of course, I excel at everything I try, as befits one of my exalted status, but Cleometry comes frightfully easily to me. It might be the pyramid thing. Perhaps next year I'll take an architecture class—then I can draw up a royally incredible bedroom makeover.   —Cleo

Oceanography, mate! Even though I grew up in the deep boo sea, there's still so much to learn. And there are so many different environments, from the icy seas of the Arctic to the mysterious Scariana Trench. I don't know that any monster will ever be able to know everything about it, and that makes it extra-interesting to me.

   —Lagoona

Any class that is fun, that challenges me and teaches me something new every day...so, all of them. ;) I don't know how you ghouls can bear to choose.
   —Ghoulia

NAME: Frankie
FAV TEACHER & WHY: I love Ms. Kindergrübber! Even though she can be scary-strict in Home Ick class, she's always there with a needle and thread to stitch me back together when I fall apart.

Ms. Kindergrübber

NAME: Draculaura
FAV TEACHER & WHY: I just adore working with Mr. Where on school plays. He knows how to find the perfomer in every monster, and he's always fair and honest when he gives critiques. Without him, the drama department would be a total hearse wreck!

Coach Igor

Mr. Where

NAME: Lagoona
FAV TEACHER & WHY: My first day at Monster High, Coach Igor gave me my own key to the swimming pool "in case you need to refresh." I know some monsters think he's kind of rough around the edges, but he's always been scary-sweet to me...even if he does yell at practice a lot.

NAME: Clawdeen
FAV TEACHER & WHY: Ms. K is my fave, too! She's got an eye for design that's helped me out of an art slump more than once...and she sometimes lets me stay after school to use the sewing machines for my own projects.

Mr. D'Eath

NAME: Ghoulia
FAV TEACHER & WHY: Although some monsters find him morose, I enjoy talking with Mr. D'Eath. He tries to be kind and encouraging to every student, and he's completely fluent in Zombie, which makes going to him for advice all the easier.

NAME: Cleo
FAV TEACHER & WHY: Mr. Mummy. Although Clawculus is not my strongest subject, he is as patient as the tomb when explaining concepts to...certain monsters who may not grasp things right away. It helps that he is an eons-old friend of my family as well.

Mr. Mummy

Extra-special shout-out to Headless Headmistress Bloodgood... I don't know if she counts as a teacher but I think we can all agree she's the beast headmistress Monster High could have! :)

Headmistress Bloodgood

Totes McGhost! She has pulled our stitches out of the fire more times than I can count!

SCHOOL UNLIFE

When I'm not helping my ghoulfriends, I volunteer as one of Headless Headmistress Bloodgood's student helpers. It really opened my eyes to how much work goes into running Monster High! —Frankie

STUDENT HELPER

Drama club. Someone as magnificent as myself simply cannot pass up an opportunity to seek the spotlight whenever possible. —Cleo

I admit it is a bit like herding werecats at times, but I love this school and all its students. I wouldn't wish for my unlife to be different in any way.
—Headmistress Bloodgood

DRAMA CLUB

Yeah, I'd say "drama" does sound just purr-fect for you, Cleo.
—Toralei

I find I really excel at Quiz Boo-wl. I quite enjoy "geeking out" over trivia with my teammates, and showing off our extensive knowledge on subjects ranging from Biteology to Trigular Calcometry. You would be surprised how heated the battles get, although apparently shouting "eat my coffin dust" in Ancient Manticore is considered unsportsmanlike.
—Ghoulia

QUIZ BOO-WL

PHOT-OGRE-PHY

If I picked something other than fearleading it would be newspaper Club. I like to wander around Monster High with my camera and capture photos for the stories in the Gory Gazette. Sometimes I even tag along with Spectra to take pics for her Ghost post!   —Draculaura

It's always creeperific to have a ghoulfriend help me hunt down my next story, especially one who can capture such great photos to go with it.   —Spectra

DANCE

Nothing quiiiiite compares to slipping my fins under the water. But I do love to dance even if I don't do it so much anymore, well not since, oh never mind...   —Lagoona

FASHION ENTREPRENEUR'S CLUB

Fashion Entrepreneur's Club. I founded it last scaremester and it's been great to recruit other fangtastic artists and future fashion divas—Jinafire Long, Skelita Calaveras, and Wydowna Spider are all members now, and brainstorming cutting-edge haunt couture and sharing our ideas and inspiration is scary fun.
                    —Clawdeen

FAVORITE SCHOOL SPORT
TO SCREAM ABOUT

I'm enjoying the Batball team this year, but soccer is in my blood. I've played it with my brothers and sisters since I was a cub, and the fact that the coach lets me play with my clawsome modified open-toed platform cleats is just a bonus. The opposing team might laugh at my fabulous footwear, but scoring a few goals on them wipes the smiles right off their faces. ;) —Clawdeen

As much as I enjoy acting as manager, assistant coach, and referee for many of Monster High's sports teams, my favorite sport in which to actively participate is Dodgeball. I may not be the strongest player, but I have a knack for calculations that can wipe the opposing team off the field in mere moments. —Ghoulia

Not the strongest player? Whatever, ghoul—you've got the most accurate arm on the team and it's howlingly obvious that your mad skills can't be underestimated. I still remember the first time I played against you—I made the mistake of ignorin' you and you took me out in the first round like it was no big fang. Now when we play, I make sure to pick you first. :) —Clawd

Oh my ghoul, I like watching (and playing) soooo many sports, from Graveball to Skultimate Roller Maze. And every Monster High team is voltageous, so it's impossible for me to choose a favorite. Give me another century or so and maybe I'll be able to narrow it down... —Frankie

Do I even need to say it? Swim Team. The water is where I feel most at home. I really love my teammates, too—there's so many different types of monsters on the team, and that diversity makes us great! —Lagoona

I never thought I'd say this, but Skultimate Roller Maze is, like, the most fun I've had in my unlife! I still get bats in my stomach before every match, but when I'm out on the track, I feel totally invincible!   —Draculaura

It's certainly a scaredevil sport—but you excel at it most admirably, my friend! —Robecca

I prize my role as Fear Squad team captain. It's one area where I've definitively outshone my older sister Nefera, a.k.a. she-who-thinks-she's-soooo-great. Our win at Monster Mashionals made her royally jealous for months...not that I noticed, of course. —Cleo

NAME: Frankie

How can I forget my first day at Monster High? I was totally nervous about being the new ghoul at school, but you all made me feel welcome right away, despite my clumsy start. Meeting all of you ghouls was the beast day of my unlife. <3

NAME: Draculaura

Landing the lead in the school play! I mean, I didn't even clawdition— Mr. Where just saw my potential and asked me to step in. I was so flattered, and I think I did a good job...even though I had bats in my stomach the entire time.

NAME: Clawdeen

The day we staged the fashion flash-mob at school. You ghouls helped me to pull off the haunt couture coup of the century—and scored me a ticket to Scaris, the fashion capital of the monster world! I'll never forget how clawsome that felt.

NAME: Cleo

I admit, the day Frankie convinced Draculaura and Clawdeen to join the Fear Squad is a good memory for me. When Toralei quit and took the rest of the team with her, I thought I was up the Nile river without a Charon...but Frankie saved the day. Even if it took MONTHS of grueling practice to get you ghouls up to my standards.

NAME: Lagoona

Freeing the frogs from the science lab was finsane—but totally worth it. I couldn't let those poor little green guys be dissected. Fortunately you ghouls had my back, and now the little guys are hopping free in the school pond. <3 A happy ending for everyone except Mr. Hack. He had to have us dissect toy frogs instead. ;)

NAME: Ghoulia

Winning my first dodgeball tournament. I "rule" quite often at skullastics, but triumphing in an athletic setting was a special moment for me. It was wonderful to have the support of the other monsters on the team as well.

$$mh + 0^2 = boo!$$

I like to find a classmate in Study Howl and see if they want to review the material together. That way I can see if there are any holes in my notes—and teaching someone else always charges me up!

—Frankie

I usually study in the bathtub. Don't laugh! A nice, relaxing soak in a scented bubble bath makes it easier for me to soak up knowledge, too. :P

—Draculaura

Sharing a room with my little sis Howleen makes it tough to study at home. I usually take my iCoffin loaded with my favorite tunes to the Coffin Bean and find a comfy chair to curl up and cram in. Having lots of caffeine handy helps, too.

—Clawdeen

Studying can be a snooze fest, so I usually have my servants review the text and read it out loud to me while I relax. Being a deNile does come with some perks. —Cleo

$$\Sigma'\Sigma(k)=mh^2 \sqrt{\text{🦇}} = \{m+h\}$$

...with Clawdeen—
...e Coffin Bean is
...fantastic study
...ot free from
...st distractions...
...us I can usually
...ount on meeting
...ne of you ghouls
...here to help me. :)
—Lagoona

I make a schedule of subjects I need to review, factoring in breaks every hour to prevent boo-redom. My favorite study spot is my desk at home, where I have optimal light, multiple seating arrangements, and copious amounts of brain food on hand. —Ghoulia

NAME THREE THINGS

LURKING IN YOUR LOCKER

SCHOOL UNLIFE

Frankie

1. A battery charger for when I get run down in the afternoons
2. The fearleading practice schedule, so I can be sure I'm never late
3. Extra needle and thread for, um, accidents

Draculaura

Only three things?? You ghouls KNOW how much I keep in my locker! Okay...
1. My makeup bag for those little between-class touch-ups
2. My writing die-ary
3. A bottle of SPF 500 sunscream. Never leave the coffin without it!

Clawdeen

1. My latest sketchbook
2. My monster hairbrush
3. A back-up razor for those fearsome full moons. Talk about bad fur days...Ugh.

Don't worry, you always look totally fierce, Clawdeen! ;)

Yeah, but being this fabulous takes hard work!

Cleo

1. A fold-out full-length mirror
2. A full complement of dynastically gore-geous accessories in case I need to change my look...
3. Spare bandages. A mummy is never fully dressed without her regal wrappings.

Ghoulia

1. My scooter helmet (and one for Sir Hoots-a-Lot, too)
2. My personalized dodgeball
3. An extra set of glasses in case something unfortunate happens to my current pair. I'm blind as a bat without them, metaphorically speaking.

Lagoona

1. Fish food for Neptuna
2. A spare suit for swim practice
3. A scary amount of monsturizer. ;P I don't always have time to hit the pool between classes.

SCHOOL UNLIFE

NAME: Frankie

FAV FOOD & WHY: The boosagna is shockingly good! I should ask to get the recipe for the monsteranara sauce they use—I bet it would taste great on my mom's spaghetti boo-lognese, too!

NAME: Draculaura

FAV FOOD & WHY:

I can always sink my fangs into some fresh veggies from the salad bar—especially after Frankie and I give it a re-vamp. Having lots of options to munch at lunch is the beast!

NAME: Clawdeen

FAV FOOD & WHY: Screechzza is usually a safe choice—just be careful that the monsterella cheese doesn't bite back.

NAME: Cleo
FAV FOOD & WHY:

The soft-serve eye-scream is always an icy treat—strawscarry vanilla swirl is my favorite. Don't listen to Toralei, though—I did NOT throw a "royal hissy fit" when the machine was out of order last week.

Yes, you did! —Toralei

NAME: Lagoona

FAV FOOD & WHY: The ghoulash is delish, but it sits in your stomach like a tombstone! I made the mistake of eating it before swim practice once and nearly sank to the infinite bottom of the pool's deep end. Mortalfying, but worth it.

NAME: Ghoulia
FAV FOOD & WHY: The tarantuladas that the lurch ladies tested out last year were quite delicious. The downside was that they contained so much grrlic that none of the vampire students could venture near the creepateria for a week!

IT'S A STONE-COLD BUMMER THEY WON'T MAKE A REAPPEARANCE. THEY REALLY WERE MONSTROUSLY GOOD.
—DEUCE

Frankie

My gingerdead cookies are the beast. Baking reminds me a lot of Mad Science—you have to get the proportions just right, or you end up with a monster mess. Ms. Kindergrübber even said that mine taste scary-close to her home-cooked recipe, which had me practically bursting at the seams with pride.

> You can count on mε to bε your kitchεn Igor anytimε, Frankiε!
> —Jackson

Draculaura

Vegetable stir-fright with ghost peppers. My family's spicy secret recipe! I substitute tofu crumble for the growled beef and even Clawd can't tell the difference. ;)

Clawdeen

My big sis Clawdia sent me an authentic Londoom recipe for fangers and mash. It was a monster hit in class, and it was so scary-easy to make! I can't wait to try it out on her the next time she visits home.

Cleo

Pyramid pi. And no, that's not a misspelling—it's geometrically sound and dynastically delectable. Alas, it's so gore-geous that it's almost a crime to slice it up for serving!

These all sound smokin'! How about you ghouls make these and I'll taste test which is the beast? -Heath

Lagoona

Dragon noodle soup makes for fintastic comfort food. My mum uses kelp noodles in her recipe, so that's how I make it, too—I think it makes it extra-healthy and tasty, too!

Ghoulia

Boofflés are my forté. You must be patient and quiet, especially while the boofflé rises, or else you will end up with flat lumps instead of fluffy treats. Slow and steady is my recipe for success.

FANG-TASTIC FIELD TRIP

SCHOOL UNLIFE

I was totally hooked on our trip to the ascarium—the whole thing was a scream, especially since I'd never been before. Who would have thought there were so many creepy-cute animals under the sea? I especially loved petting the electric eels—we got along voltageously! Although Toralei did cause a little trouble in the Great Scarrier Reef exhibit... —Frankie

We took a scary-long time to break for lunch and that place is like the world's biggest sushi buffet. How's a kitty supposed to control herself? Besides, they wouldn't even let me eat one itty-bitty fish...talk about stingy. —Toralei

The trip to Lake Eerie was a surprisingly wonderful outing! The lake was flat and calm—monstrously different from the rough tide I'm used to surfing! —Lagoona

The Unnatural History Museum is just clawsome—maybe it's a wolf thing, but I get a real kick out of looking at old bones. I was glad that my siblings weren't along for the trip, though—knowing Clawd, he would have tried to take one home to bury in the backyard. —Clawdeen

Sitting next to Deuce and watching the sky-show unfold at the PlanetScarium reminded me of our trip to Boo York, back when comet fever was in full swing. With all that happened the evening of the gala, we never really got to watch the skies together—but sitting in the dark and seeing the stars projected overhead onto the big dome, I held his hand and felt like I got a royal do-over. He really is the love of my unlife. <3 —Cleo

There is a wonderful romance in the night sky. I hope I can help Manny see that someday, too! —Iris

The Monsterpolitan Museum of Art was to. die. for. It's soooo scaremazing to stand in front of a painting by a famous artist like Vincent van Ghost or Clawed Moanet and actually see every teeny-tiny brushstroke for yourself. I could fang out there for hours and hours trying to figure out their techniques!
—Draculaura

The city li-bury is most definitely my favorite. Our school li-bury is fine, but I prefer stacks that I can shuffle around in for hours and hours...not to mention archives with books dating back centuries!
—Ghoulia

MUST WEAR ON
SCHOOL PICTURE DAY!

SCHOOL UNLIFE

NAME: Frankie
WHAT TO WEAR: A truly electrifying outfit! I like to mix and match bold colors and patterns until I find a combo that sparks my interest...And then I change my mind about ten times before I come back to my original choice. Sigh.

NAME: Draculaura
WHAT TO WEAR: Fangtastic accessories are a must for me since I'm a vampire. I never show up in photos, so I have to make sure what the camera does see is 100% fa-boo-lous! Cute hair pins and freaky-chic earrings help me feel extra visible.

NAME: Clawdeen
WHAT TO WEAR: I usually pick out my most fiercely fashionable top and build the rest of the day's wardrobe around it. Bright colors and lots of flashy accessories help me stand out from the pack.

NAME: Cleo
WHAT TO WEAR: My servants end hours making sure that my hair and makeup is absolutely FLAWLESS. If I am to be immortalized in a photo, I simply must look my best—and that means not even one hair on my head can be out of place.

NAME: Lagoona
WHAT TO WEAR: My style is usually way casual but on picture day I like to kick it up with something a little more fashion-forward while still staying true to my laid-back lurk. ;) Comfy but chic is my rule!

NAME: Ghoulia
WHAT TO WEAR: The perfect pair of spook-tacles makes for a spectacular school photo for me. I have many geeky-chic pairs of glasses to choose from, and I select my outfit to match my favorite fierce frames.

FAVORITE FEARLEADING CHEER

SCHOOL UNLIFE

Monster High, stomp your feet!
We're the team that can't be beat!
Screech and howl and moan and roar!
Come on team, push up that score!
—Frankie

From the East to the West
Our Nightmares are the best
Monsters shriek and shout
We're gonna knock you out!
Gooooo Nightmares!
—Draculaura

V-I-C-T-O-R-Y
That's our monster battle cry!
And when we S-C-O-R-E
Six feet under's where you'll be!
—Clawdeen

Monster High's got royal spirit!
Monster High's got royal style!
You know that when you hear it
We beat you by a royal mile!
—Cleo

Backstroke, breaststroke,
butterfly, free!
We're coming in like a tsunami!
Kick your feet or wiggle your fin
We're the team that's gonna win!
—Lagoona

Secant, cosine, tangent, sine
Three point one four one five nine
Add the remainder, carry the two
I calculate that we'll beat you!
—Ghoulia

GO TEAM!!!

SCHOOL MUSICAL

YOU'RE UN-DYING TO STAR IN

SCHOOL UNLIFE

West Side Gory for sure! The story totes tugs my heartstrings and the songs are creeperifically catchy. I loooove the costumes—retro, but not T retro, you know? I'm pretty sure I still have most of those outfits in the back of my closet somewhere.
—Draculaura

The Wonderful Wizard of Claws seems like it would be totally voltageous! With my incredible detachable limbs, I'd be a shoe-in for the scarecrow.
—Frankie

Furspray! Clawsome dancing and a story that's all about being yourself and fighting for others' rights? I'd be over the moon to land that part. —Clawdeen

Werecats! but i would be purrfect in any role where I am center stage.
—Toralei

The Thing and I.
The leading role is a majestic ruler who is always, always right— why, it's almost as if it was written just for me!
—Cleo

South Clawcific
Sometimes a ghoul has to sing about washing that manster right out of her hair... but then take him back before curtain call ;)
—Lagoona

It had always been my dream to star in the school musical, and this year I was finally chosen for the lead role in Screaming in the Drain. It was a surprising smash— thanks in no small part to my co-star, Catty.
—Ghoulia

It was a total blast! I loved being in the supporting role for once. And you were just fangtastic as the lead! I can't wait to clawdition alongside you next year. —Catty

IN THE FEARBOOK
YOU'D BE VOTED MOST
LIKELY TO...

I NOMINATE: Frankie

I nominate Frankie for "most likely to help out a ghoulfriend." I will never forget how she helped me rescue mon amor, Garrott, from the Catacombs of Scaris. Her willingness to go above and beyond for her friends c'est merveilleux! —Rochelle

Aww, I always try to be the most helpful monster I can be. Even if it backfires sometimes... okay, a lot of the time. But I try! —Frankie

I NOMINATE: Draculaura

Draculaura would definitely win "most likely to cry at a romantic boovie." I can practically set my watch by her waterworks. It's creepy cute, to be honest. ;)
—Clawd

I wouldn't mind winning "cutest couple" with you, Clawd! :) —Draculaura

I NOMINATE: Clawdeen

Clawdeen is "most likely to be a famous fashionista" without a doubt. Her burning passion is an inspiration to all monsters. —Jinafire

That means a lot coming from you, Jinafire—your passion for fashion burns just as bright as mine! —Clawdeen

I NOMINATE: Cleo

Cleo's organizational skills, monstrous confidence, and fierce determination make her "most likely to rule the world," at least by my calculations. —Ghoulia

And your calculations are nearly as flawless as I am. Of course, ruling the world might cut into my "me-time," but one does have to make sacrifices for the good of the common people... —Cleo

I NOMINATE: Lagoona

Of all the students at Monster High, I think Lagoona wins "most likely to compete at the Howlympics," claws-down! Her swim team records are unbeatable, and she's got the determination to power through any obstacle. —Gil

With monsters who boo-lieve in me as much as you do, Gil, how can I possibly fail? :) —Lagoona

I NOMINATE: Ghoulia

With her brains, she could do anything she'd like, but Ghoulia is definitely "most likely to become a mad scientist." She'll end up saving the world with her scary smarts, mark my words. —Cleo

I do wish to help monsterkind with scientific achievements... and it helps to know that my royal beastie has my back. :) —Ghoulia

Frankie

Oh my ghoul, it's so hard to choose! I think I've liked just about every movie I've seen. Um, I guess if you twisted my arm, I'd pick Frightanic. It's just so romantic. And thrilling. And tragic. I cried so much last time I watched it that I nearly gave myself a short-circuit!

Draculaura

Can I pick all six of the Vampire Majesty movies? I know it's a tiny bit cliché, but forbitten romance totally puts bats in my belfrey. <3 Plus, I can watch my friend Elissabat—or as she's better known, Veronica Von Vamp—light up the silver scream with her acting talent.

I know what you mean...a good star-crossed love story is just the best! —Lagoona

Clawdeen

Breakfast at Griffiny's, for sure! I swear Audrey Creepburn is the most gore-geous and talented actress in monster history. Plus, Edith Headless's costumes are fab-u-lous. When I'm running my fangtastic fashion empire I will SO be taking time out to moonlight as a costume designer.

Cleo

I have a weakness for Clawrence of Scarabia. The magnificence of the desert cannot be overstated, and the story is epic enough even for my royal eyes. (It also might make me a tiiiiny bit homesick for Egypt... just a tiny, tiny bit, though.)

Lagoona

My favorite is Boo Crush. Three ghoulfriends, surfing monster waves all over Clawaii and trying to be the best without losing sight of good sportsmanship—I can totally relate. Plus, I'm dying to surf Horrorkipa Beach someday!

Ghoulia

Deadfast 4: Terminal Velocity currently occupies the #1 spot in my esteem. That's not to say that the older Deadfast movies do not have their merits, but some of the special effects look very dated by today's standards, and the dialogue can be downright campy. Of course, I do rather prefer Tobey Armbiter's performance from the first film...hmmm. Perhaps I should re-assess.

...und these totally frightastic
...aps from our trip to Hauntly-
...ood! You ghouls look boo-tiful.
...d so does my camerawork ;)

Honey

Halloween is a total scream! Sure, it used to be a scary day for monsterkind, because normies were scared of us, but now it's a chance for fearious monster-normie bonding! And wearing awesome costumes and eating lots and lots of candy...gosh, now I'm sparking at the bolts for next year! —Frankie

Boo Year's Eve is totes my fave. Something about the change in the air and having the chance to put bad blood behind you just gets me pumped! The parties are creeptastic, too—staying up past midnight, sharing that Boo Year kiss with your special someone, and then getting together to sing Auld Fang Syne...I hope I have 1600 more just like it! —Draculaura

My whole family—brothers, sisters, aunts, uncles, cousins—come in from all over for a monster feast at Fangsgiving. Cooking enough food to feed everyone is an epic undertaking, but I gotta say, it really brings the whole pack together. At least until it's time to fight over the last piece of pie...
—Clawdeen

MONSTER HIGH

Valentide's Day is a day when sea monsters exchange gifts with the ones they love most. It's a saltwater tradition, but Gil has started celebrating it with me every year, even though he's freshwater. He always surprises me with monstrously thoughtful gifts, too—like a cosmetics kit I'd had my eye on for ages, or a scary-expensive wax for my surfboard. It just shows how much he scares about me. <3 —Lagoona

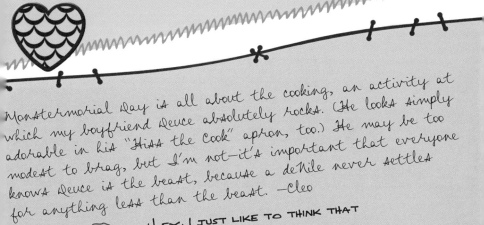

Monstermorial Day is all about the cooking, an activity at which my boyfriend Deuce absolutely rocks. (He looks simply adorable in his "Kiss the Cook" apron, too.) He may be too modest to brag, but I'm not—it's important that everyone knows Deuce is the beast, because a deNile never settles for anything less than the beast. —Cleo

HEY, I JUST LIKE TO THINK THAT SCARY—DELICIOUS FOOD IS ITS OWN REWARD. —DEUCE

Zombies often do not get the respect we deserve in the monster world—that is why Zombiependence Day is such an important part of my scaritage. We eat zombie food and sing traditional zombie songs, like "Uuuugh" and "Ooaaargh Uuunngh." My favorite part is lighting the fireworks...and then running away from them very, very slowly. —Ghoulia

I know Clawdeen will think I'm way weird, but I LOVE to fang at her place. It's fun to see what it'd be like to have a big family like hers! I'd really like to have a couple of siblings myself, but every time I bring up the possibility of a new brother or sister my parents get REALLY embarrassed for some reason. —Frankie

The park! I know, I know, you'd think vampire + sunlight = monstrously bad news, but I just bring a nice big umbrella and some sunscream and I'm good to go. It's the best place to get in a good poetry writing sesh—plus I can always play fetch with Clawd. ;) —Draculaura

The Maul, of course. No one beats this wolf to a sale—I can sniff out a monster deal on Alexander McScream and Louis Creton faster than you can bli Refreshing my wardrobe is my favorite way to relax. —Clawd

The die-ner is just the beast. The swim team and I go there after practice to fang out and gnash on some of their famous booberry pie. The tomb-box they have is loaded with the latest fintastic hits, too, which makes it hard to resist getting up from the booth and turning the die-ner into a dance floor!   —Lagoona

I must agree with Clawdeen, it's hard to deny the allure of the Maul. There's nothing better than being waited on hand and foot by store lurks dying to make a sale. After all, anything I buy is guaranteed to become THE haunt new item. —Cleo

The food corpse at the Maul is by far my favorite haunt. So many varieties of fast food within a few easy steps of each other, and no one to moan at you for taking up a table. Also, there is free wi-fi, so I can play games on my iCoffin or surf the web while I feast on my favorite brain food. —Ghoulia

The coffin bean. Nothing like curling up with a catnipucino and listening in on other monsters' conversations! —Toralei

FAVORITE
GHOULS' NIGHT OUT
ACTIVITY

NAME: Frankie
FAV GNO ACTIVITY:
I love it when my ghouls and I have a chance to hit a concert— seeing a big star like Casta Fierce performing live gets me all kinds of charged up! There's something energizing about fanging in a monster crowd with your beast friends, too. <3

NAME: Draculaura
FAV GNO ACTIVITY:
Seeing a boovie on opening night is totes my fave. Especially when it stars my friend Elissabat—I mean, Veronica Von Vamp. ;) And ever since we got back from Hauntlywood ... a much better ...ation for all ...rk that ...ehind the ...er scream.

$15	100	07	2	EI
ADMISSION	SECTION	ROW	SEAT	
$3.00				
100	MH PRODUCTIONS PRESENTS		1	
78RT768	**CASTA FIERCE**		ADU	
	LOCATION			
07	**MONSTER AUDITORIUM**		07	
0ZX7 0Z	DATE		15	
2	**OCTOBER 31ST**		2	
XIO2105	LOWER LEVEL		009FL	

Casta Fierce

NAME: Cleo
FAV GNO ACTIVITY: I like to put together our most magnificent outfits and go dancing. What's the point of getting all wrapped up in your finest if you're not going to be seen and admired? Bonus if Holt Hyde is deejaying—he really heats up the dance floor.

NAME: Clawdeen

FAV GNO ACTIVITY: Howling along to the hits with your BFFs at scary-oke is always a blast—especially when we can convince our new friend Catty Noir to come along. She may be taking a break from being a super-famous pop idol, but the ghoul is still a spooktacular singer.

It's so un-boo-lievable that a monster that used to sell out stadium concerts attends Monster High with us now. She's such a sweet, kind ghoul, too—although I still bloom with excitement every time I see her in the hallways. —Venus

NAME: Lagoona

FAV GNO ACTIVITY: Art ghouleries are fintastically fun especially with your friends in tow. Grazing on horror d'oeuvres and checking out the newest wave of upcoming artists is a gnashing way to pass the time with your mates.

NAME: Ghoulia

FAV GNO ACTIVITY: When it's my turn to choose, my ghouls and I will hit up the scarcade for some creeperific fun. You would be surprised how uhh-mazing we are at Dance or Die—no one else can nail the Zombie Shake like me.

FAVORITE PLACE TO SHOP

Any store that sells accessories. My dad gives me a biiiig sigh whenever I buy new outfits—he's always complaining that my closet takes up too much space, when I swear he hasn't changed his style since the 16th century. But he won't say boo if I come home with a necklace and matching earrings. ;)
—Draculaura

For a sea monster on dry land like me, skin care is serious business! But that doesn't mean it has to be a chore. I'm always browsing cosmetics counters for new monsturizing makeup to help me stay hydrated—especially if it's glittery or comes in a cute case, or smells extra-ghoulicious...
—Lagoona

My new friend Bonita Femur has turned me on to Ghoul Will! It's a great place for refreshing your lurk when you don't want to spend too much money. You'd be shocked at the cute stuff I've found there—and with my freaky-fast sewing skills, I'm good at transmonsterfying even a shabby old outfit into something drop-dead gorgeous! —Frankie

Always happy to help! Now if I can just stop snacking on my sleeves when I get nervous...
—Bonita

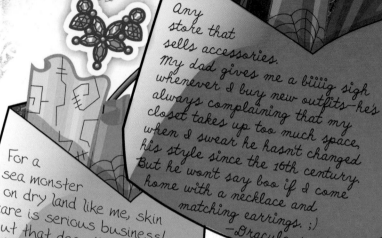

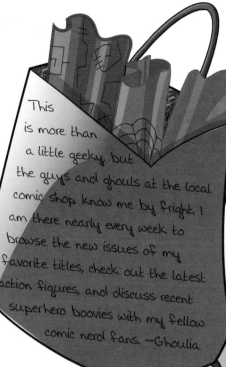

This is more than a little geeky but the guys and ghouls at the local comic shop know me by fright. I am there nearly every week to browse the new issues of my favorite titles, check out the latest action figures, and discuss recent superhero boovies with my fellow comic nerd fans. —Ghoulia

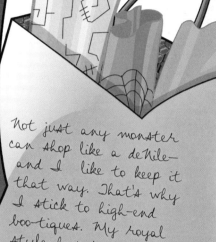

Not just any monster can shop like a deNile—and I like to keep it that way. That's why I stick to high-end boo-tiques. My royal style has to be fresh and ALWAYS one step ahead of the commoners. —Cleo

Oh my ghoul, I'm not sure if shoe stores are my favorite, or if they're the wolfsbane of my existence. I can't go to the Maul without picking up a freaky-fab new pair. Sometimes I wonder where my allowance goes, and then I look at my shoe tree and I remember. ;P (At least Howleen has finally grown out of chewing them to pieces.) —Clawdeen

Hey! I only did that, like, twice. >:| Three times at the most. —Howleen

NAME: Draculaura
FAV FAM THING & WHY:

Now that I've finally gotten all of my vampire powers, Daddy has taken me under his wing so I can earn my flying license! I love spending time with him, although he's SUCH a backseat flyer. "Blah! Draculaura, put your echolocation on! Draculaura, don't scare the real bats! Blah, did you put your wing signal on back there? Blah! BLAH!" At least our batty bonding time has made us closer.

NAME: Frankie
FAV FAM THING & WHY: I think sometimes my parents are bummed that I was never really a little ghoul, so they sometimes can't help but treat me like one. Last weekend they took me to the playunderground. I'm a teenager, so it was kiiind of embarrassing, but fanging out with my parents on a nice day is still voltage. Also, being pushed on the swingset is actually REALLY fun! <3

NAME: Clawdeen
FAV FAM THING & WHY: Fanging out at Black Lake. My parents used to take my siblings and me there when we were cubs, and lately we've started up the tradition again. Picnicking, paddling around in the water, jumping off of the cliffs, and sunning on the rocky shore...it's so much fun that my sibs and I can forget we're related and get along for a little while. ;)

Being silly with my sibs!

NAME: Ghoulia

FAV FAM THING & WHY:

Every Frightday is game night in the Yelps household. We play Monsteropoly, Rotzee, the Game of Unlife...but our favorite by far is Terror-vial Pursuit. It takes us each about a minute to reach over and hit the buzzer, but it is always a gripping race to see who will get to chime in first!

NAME: Cleo

FAV FAM THING & WHY:

Any family time that doesn't involve Nefera is a scream come true. I do love spending time with my daddy-mummy, but when my monstrous model sister is around, she takes up all of his attention, when his attention should rightfully be on ME.

NAME: Lagoona

FAV FAM THING & WHY: This might surprise you, but we Blues love to sit in for a knit-in! Fishnet and loose knit go together like marmite and toast, after all. Working together with waterproof thread, we can create freaky-fab knitwear for my fishy fiends. As my mum likes to say, "There's always purls in the ocean!" ;)

You and I need to sit down for some creature crafting time! Knitting comes naturally to me, for some reason.
        —Wydowna

At first I thought dating Deuce meant tolerating the classic rock he's always blasting...but I admit I've come to love it, too. Although I have to hide my iCoffin from daddy-mummy—he say that any music that can't be played on reed instruments by servants isn't proper music for a Pharaoh. —Cleo

Ever since I got back from Madread, I have been listening to loads of salsa and merengue music. I love the fancy finned footwork—but I do have to explain to some monsters that they are dances and not food. —Lagoona

My tastes are a teensy bit flighty—I tend to get wayyyyy into popular groups and then drop them when the next big fang comes along. It's a weakness, but I've seen so many groups and singers come and go over 1600 years that it's hard for me to get staked down to just one. ;) Right now, my favorites are definitely Catty Noir and Casta Fierce—they're the hottest acts on the monster music scene! —Draculaura

Rhythm & boos. I always have a project going, and there's nothing like a catchy tune with a monster bassline to ramp up my pace! Plus, rhythm & boos is full of fashionistas so far ahead of the creepy curve it's like they're from the future. Watching their vids online makes for clawsome inspiration. —Clawdeen

Holt has totally gotten me into dance music. Anything with an electrifying beat really gets me all charged up! Sometimes literally—when his monster DJ equipment blows a fuse, my bolts and I are there to make sure the show can always go on! —Frankie

GOOD TO KNOW I CAN COUNT ON YOU TO KEEP MY SQUEALS OF STEEL TURNING, FRANKIE-FINE! —HOLT

You would not think so, but Boograss is a surprisingly technical and complicated style of music that greatly appeals to me. It takes a dead-icated monster to play it well, and a good band must be able to read one another so well that they might as well be psychic— which some of them are. —Ghoulia

I had no idea you were a Boograss fan, ghoul! Creep down to the catacombs sometime and we can listen to some of my favorite bands together. I have GOT to introduce you to psychobilly—you will un-die! —Operetta

FAVORITE THING
TO DO AT A CREEPOVER

FAVES

Ghoul talk! We read magazines like Monster Beat and Teen Scream and talk about the latest fashion trends, our skelebrity crushes, and who's our favorite contestant on Next Top Monster. Sometimes fanging out and doing nothing is the beast way to get to know your ghoulfriends. —Frankie

Makeovers, of course! I love doing my friends' hair and makeup and letting them try out new lurks on me—I just wish I could see the results with my own eyes. At least I trust my friends not to take embarrassing photos of me and post them online or something. :
— Draculaura

It's not a real creepover without truth or scare— as long as you never cross over into mean ghoul territory. I know which of my BFFs can take a little teasing, and I'm always on guard to make sure it never gets out of paw. I wouldn't want to lose any of my ghoulfriends over a dare, after all.

— Clawdeen

It's no secret that I rule at games. Gargoyles to Gargoyles is my favorite— although it's gotten much more fun now that everyone's stopped just letting me win. Even a deNile appreciates a challenge, just as long as everyone bows to my superiority eventually.
—Cleo

Cannot wait for rematch. I will, how you say, kick your butt. ;) —Abbey

Oh, it is on!!

Mani-pedis are scary-fun—some of my mates have long claws and toenails that just beg for a monstrous makeover. And if you mess up, no worries—you can always just start over with a brand new color.   —Lagoona

Scary normie movies are a must for any creepover. Booing the villain, throwing popcorn when the hero says a silly one-liner, shrieking at the jump scares... when you are surrounded by your beast friends, even being a scaredy-ghoul can be feariously enjoyable.   —Ghoulia

FAVS

MONSTER HIGH

This summer I went camping for the very first time! My parents thought it would be a creepycool experience for me, and it was totally fun—although building the campfire was tough because Dad kept yelling "Fire bad!" and putting it out. Still, I can't wait to go again—and bring my ghoulfriends next time!
—Frankie

Vacations to glamorous locations are the pinnacle of my summer—my father travels quite often and he feels that I am mature enough to accompany him as long as it doesn't interfere with my own grueling social schedule. Scaris, Plague, Madread...travel to exotic locales is exciting even for royalty. —Cleo

Summer is a fangtastic time to get organized for the next year! I always make time to go through my closet and clear out the outfits I know I won't wear again. It can take quite awhile, since my closet is full of 1600 years of fashion! I make sure to give the coolest stuff to my friends, or donate it to Ghoul Will, so it doesn't go to waste. —Draculaura

A hard-working ghoul like me never rests, even during summer vacation—I work like a mad wolf on my fashion designs and sewing skills. I'm thinking about trying to scare up an internship next summer, so I can get my claws in the industry! —Clawdeen

When I get back from visiting my family in Fanghai, we should get together and brainstorm new lurks. Talking with you always lights my creative fire.
—Jinafire

My favorite part of summer is taking a trip back home to visit my friends from down under. I love Monster High, but I'd be lying if I said I never missed my old mates from middle school—it's good to float around with them and catch up.
<3 —Lagoona

I haven't actually done it yet, but my dearest wish this summer is to be able to attend Nekrocon. To talk with my favorite artists and writers, see trailers for upcoming boovies, and buy all sorts of exclusive geeky "swag"—ahh, it sounds like nerdvana! —Ghoulia

A CERTAIN ZOMBIE MAY HAVE ALREADY BOUGHT OUR TICKETS FOR NEXT YEAR...AS WELL AS VIP PASSES FOR THE DEADFAST PANEL. ;) —SLO MO

Although it is an anatomical improbability, I think my brain may have just exploded from joy. Best. Boyfriend. Ever.

That I didn't fall to pieces so easily. Being flexible isn't so bad, but you can't let yourself fly apart at every little thing! —Frankie

A closet that NEVER gets full! Or one that always has the perfect outfit waiting in it...either way, Dad would stop driving me batty about how much stuff I have. —Draculaura

I've had some bad experiences with careless wishing before, so I'd just wish that my mates find happiness with who they are. Because they're all fintastic already! —Lagoona

I'm still so sorry about that, Lagoona. :(I didn't know that wishing Gil's parents would like you would turn you into a freshwater monster that was totally not you! —Howleen

No worries, mate. It all worked out for the beast in the end. <3

Wish? What would I possibly need to wish for? I'm a deNile. My unlife is as flawless as I am.
—Cleo

I'd just wish for infinite sketchbooks... the nice ones can get really expensive. What, you thought I'd wish to be a famous fashion designer? Pssh, this ghoul can make that wish come true all on her own. ;) —Clawdeen

Take it from me. Hard work and patience is the only way to really make your wishes come true the way you want them to. :)
—Gigi

To be able to speak any language... only being capable of speaking Zombie makes me a bit sad sometimes. I would love to be able to communicate with monsters all across the world!
—Ghoulia

Your wishes are so sweet! I think all of you ghouls are perfect just the way you are! I couldn't have wished for more clawsome friends! —Gigi

PICK A MAGIC POWER AND TELL US WHY

I think seeing into the future would be voltageous! I don't need to see that far ahead—just far enough to tell if I'm about to make a major mistake. My social unlife would be a lot smoother if I could tell when I'm being helpful and when I'm putting my foot in my mouth. —Frankie

Oooh, I am dying to be able to talk to animals like Jane Boolittle! Count Fabulous and I could have so many creeper conversations—I bet he could give so much good flying advice, too! And he'd be able to tell me when about to have a moth! so I can take him outsi —Draculaura

Count Fabulous says he wishes he could talk to you, too... but he loves you monstrous much. :)
—Jane

I'd like to be able to control time. Then I could speed through the deadly-boring stuff like Clawculus class and get straight to the good things, like fanging out with my ghouls or designing a new line of iconic lurks. <3 —Clawdeen

Although my father's amulets and charms have quite a lot of magic already, if I had to choose... I think I'd like to be able to create light. That way I wouldn't have to rely on a fright light at night. (Yes, I'm a monster who's afraid of the dark. Deal with it.)
—Cleo

I've always wondered what it would be like to fly. I reckon it would be just like swimming, but through the air. It would be scary-fun to be able to just drop in on my ghouls at any time—literally! —Lagoona

I would certainly want to be speedy— as quick as my fictional hero, Deadfast. I could accomplish so much, so much faster! And I think it would be fun to experience unlife at the speed of light.
—Ghoulia

Ghoulia
DEADFAST

DYING TO KNOW YOU

MY TRIP
ACCORDING
TO:
Frankie Stein

There's no way I could choose—there are just too many freaky-fabulous places to go, and I've hardly been to any of them! I want to go everywhere that I possibly can, and I don't mind in what order.

—Frankie

I've never been to the Boohamas, but I'm totally un-dying to visit because I hear the water is warm and the surfing there is totally dank! Plus, there are so many islands that a ghoul can get lost exploring them all.
                                        —Lagoona

Since I've already been to Scaris and Boo York, the haunt couture capitals of the wolrd, I've been wanting to visit Monster Picchu. The beautiful textiles and patterns have me thinking of all sorts of new designs. —Clawdeen

With your love of bright colors and fearless fashion choices, I know you will feel right at home in my colorful culture! Just promise me that if you make a Monster Picchu-inspired shoe, it will come in size 42EEE. ;)
                                        —Marisol

I've been before, briefly, but I'd love to go back to Roombai and really have a chance to explore. The desert setting, the luxurious surroundings...yes, I could definitely get used to unlife there.
—Cleo

I always thought Rotland would be really nice. Lots of creepy-cool castles to haunt out in, and the weather is overcast and rainy—in other words, very vampire-friendly! Sort of reminds me of my home back in Transylvania.
—Draculaura

Nae need for sunscream, that's for certain. Although finding food you'd like tae eat might be a wee problem. I'll have to ask ma gran if she knows a vegetarian haggis recipe...
—Lorna

Barcelgroana seems as though it would be a fascinating place to visit—it has a very complex history and rich scaritage. I would love to visit the Castle of Three Dragons and stroll down the Passeig de Scarcia, or relax on Somonstroso beach.
—Ghoulia

JUST SAY the word ANd I will be your personal tour guide—BArcelgroANA is my home ANd my heart. I will take you oN A tour of LA FeANdreNA ANd shop for delicious foods At LA BooQueriA. <3 we will have such fuN, mi AmiqA! —ViperiNe

WHAT ARE YOUR DREAMS FOR THE FUTURE?

NAME: Frankie

DREAM: The future is so big and wide-open for a monster like me...I guess I just hope I can keep learning new stuff and meeting new friends! I feel so creeptastically lucky to have the unlife that I have. I just want to keep enjoying it and take things as they come.

NAME: Lagoona

DREAM: Someday I just know I'll make it to the Howlympics—I just don't know which event I want to compete in most! Fright diving? Finchronized swimming? Or maybe a scarathon... It's so hard to decide.

NAME: Clawdeen

DREAM: You have to ask? ;) Okay, then: Clawdeen Wolf is going to be one of the greatest fashion designers in all monster history! I'll eclipse Coco Charnel and Louis Creton with my fierce fashion sense and innovative designs—and I'll make sure I design clothes that every ghoul can feel good in. <3

NAME: Draculaura

DREAM: I hope to publish a book of romantic poetry that will take the monster world by storm. I have hundreds of poems written already...I just need a frightfully good editor to help me select the very very VERY best ones. Otherwise my book would be too enormous to read!

NAME: Cleo

DREAM: As a deNile, I'm able to make nearly anything I dream a reality. Still, I suppose my biggest dream is to leave a legacy worthy of my ancestors. Heavy is the head that wears the crown...especially when she has a lot of crowned heads looking over her shoulder and waiting for her to make a monster mistake.

NAME: Ghoulia

DREAM: I have an unquantifiable number of dreams and goals, all of which I am actively working to make into a reality. My most immediate goals are to publish my Deadfast fan-comic, solve Fearmat's Last Theorem, get into the monsterversity of my choice, and quadruple-major in astro-clawculus, medicine, trigular calcometry and art.

You are so scaremazingly smart and talented, Ghoulia. I don't doubt you can make all of these happen without breaking a sweat! —Frankie

CAN DEAD FAST OUTRUN
THE RAINBOW OF DOOM?!

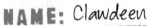

NAME: Draculaura

GIFT: The Sweet 1600 party that you ghouls threw for me! I don't think any monster could have asked for a better birthday bash. Of course, the car that my dad gave me is pretty fangtastic, too...I love driving around with Clawd in the passenger's seat, even though he can't resist sticking his head out of the window. ;)

I can't help it! It's a wolf thing. —Clawd

NAME: Clawdeen

GIFT: My first sketchbook. I got it after I'd drawn on one too many important documents when I was a cub, but it was the first sign that my family really believed in my talent. I've still got it, and even though the drawings look mortalfyingly amateurish now I keep it as a sign of how far I've come and how far I still have to go!

NAME: Frankie

GIFT: The best gift I was ever given is the first gift I was ever given—my pet Watzit! My parents gave him to me on my first day of unlife and he's been with me ever since. He's the cutest mostly-a-puppy any ghoul could ask for, and he's always there for me when I'm feeling run-down.

NAME: Cleo

GIFT: The boo-quet that Deuce gave me before our first school dance as an official couple. It was a difficult time for me. I'd just broken up with Clawd, and it felt like the whole school had turned against me because he was the Big Monster on Campus. But then Deuce showed up at my door with a dozen black roses, and I just knew I'd made the right choice. <3

NAME: Lagoona

GIFT: At the risk of sounding like a total drip, I think the chance to go to Monster High was the best gift I've ever received. I never would have met you ghouls and had so many scare-raising adventures and fantastic fun. Being up on the big dry has definitely expanded my horizons, in the best way possible.

NAME: Ghoulia

GIFT: Deadfast Issue #0. Cleo got it for me—although she doesn't know I know. ;) A lot of monsters misjudge Cleo, but she's proven to be a creeperifically caring BFF to me when it really counts.

WHAT DO YOU DO
WHEN YOU'RE BORED?

DYING TO KNOW YOU

NAME: Draculaura
BOREDOM TIP:

If I find myself with nothing to do, I'll usually try out some scream-of-consciousness writing. You clear your mind and just let your pen flow over the page. Sometimes you only come out with nonsense, but other times you can have a monster breakthrough in your writing process!

NAME: Clawdeen
BOREDOM TIP:

Try a new lurk for my hair. My fur grows freaky-fast so I can do almost anything I want, and if I don't like it it'll be back to "normal" in a few days. I'll shave half of it and dye it with purple and green tiger stripes, tease it into an afro, or just give it some gore-geous highlights.

NAME: Lagoona

BOREDOM TIP: I'll take Neptuna out for a splash in the waves so she and I can stretch our flippers. I'm never bored when I'm in the ocean, because you're never swimming in the same water twice. I think that's why I find it so easy to go with the flow most of the time, because I'm used to everything changing with the tides.

NAME: Cleo

BOREDOM TIP: I find that boredom is best solved by good company, so I text Deuce. He's usually up for fanging out, as long as he hasn't made prior plans with his buddies. If he has, then I can usually count on Ghoulia for a good Maul-crawl or ghouls' night out. She's my best friend for a reason.

NAME: Frankie

BOREDOM TIP: It's hard for me to get bored, because everything is still pretty new to me. In those rare times when I do find myself hunting for something to do, I'll usually start on a new craft project. I love to make scary-cute handmade gifts for my friends, whether it's a sweater for Clawdeen's Kitty Crescent or fin-warmers for Lagoona. Thinking about my friends always gets me charged up, too!

NAME: Ghoulia

BOREDOM TIP: I pull out a good book of brain-teasers. Exercising my gray matter easily alleviates any symptoms of idleness. (Translation: as long as I'm thinking, I'm never bored.)

Okay, first, we would take a frighteningly romantic carriage ride through the park. Then we'd go to the fanciest vegetarian restaurant in town and enjoy a five-course meal, with TWO desserts, while a violin player serenades us tableside. Then, Clawd would hold his paw out to me and ask me to dance, and we would dance the fang-dango until dawn. Oh, and I would be wearing a gore-geous dress and Clawd would be in white tie and tail. ...Um, too much?
—Draculaura

Monster Beat is always describing all kinds of dream dates for teen monsters to aspire to—but they all sound really complicated and not for me. My ideal date would probably just be something totally casual. Dinner and a boovie sounds like plenty for me right now.
—Frankie

I'm not really "doing" dating right now. But I guess if I had to pick something, I'd want to go to a full-on catwalk fashion show. Any monster who dates me should probably be just as into haunt couture as I am, otherwise they might find themselves eclipsed by my work.
—Clawdeen

My dream date is going to the Surf and Stream Expo with Gil. There's always so much to do and see, and the place holds special memories for us, because it was our third real date. We always share an order of kelp chips afterwards. It may not sound like the most romantic date, but it's special to us.
—Lagoona

My dreamiest dates are the ones where Deuce waits on me hand and and claw. Especially when he makes me a home-cooked meal and acts like chef, waiter, and monster 'd. It's so cute when he goes above and beyond to make me happy—it truly shows his dead-ication to me.
—Cleo

I am not a ghoul who demands grand romantic gestures, or is even particularly interested in such things. That said, my dream date would be to go to the amusement park and ride the fastest roller coasters and most death-defying rides. My boyfiend, Slo Mo, is fond of carnivals as well, and I'm sure we would both have a shrieking good time.
—Ghoulia

DO YOU HAVE A SECRET TALENT?

NAME: Frankie

TALENT: I'm really good at juggling! Maybe that's not such a secret, because I'm always having to juggle my bits and pieces when they decide to detach, but I can do it with regular stuff, too—gargoyle eggs, textbooks, casketballs, you name it, and I can make it fly through the air with the greatest of ease. :)

NAME: Draculaura

TALENT: Embroidery! I picked it up on a really boring weekend in the last century, and it was so scary-fun that I never really stopped. I admit it's not a skill that comes in handy that often, but at least I can put cute designs on Count Fabulous's outfits. <3

NAME: Clawdeen

TALENT: It's weird and not at all useful, but I can totally draw with my toes. Kinda good, too—I mean, it's nothing compared to how I draw with my paws, but it's a neat trick that I can whip out if I ever wear out my fingers with sketching or something.

NAME: Cleo

TALENT: I can charm snakes. It's a mummy thing...and no, before you ask, I have never used it on Deuce. Why would I need to? It might come in handy next time I meet his cousin Viperine, though—her snakes are much less well-behaved.

i know, i know...their love bites are a bad habit. :(if it makes you feel any better, though, it DOES mean that they like you as much as i do—which is a lot! —viperine

NAME: Lagoona

TALENT: I can imitate the sound of the ocean's surf so perfectly that if you close your eyes, you might think you're standing on a breezy beach! Ditto with dripping water—almost any kind of watery sound, actually. I guess it's because I've spent so much time there.

$$\Sigma\Sigma(k)=mh^2$$
$$\frac{\triangleright i(e)k}{mh}$$

NAME: Ghoulia

TALENT: Reciting pi to the ten-thousandth decimal place. It is not exactly a talent that is in high demand, though, since it takes a couple of hours to get that far out loud. I could possibly go further, but rote memorization is not as interesting to me as discovering something new.

WHAT'S YOUR ORDER AT THE COFFIN BEAN?

An iced scaramel latte and a booberry muffin. Extra booberries, please!
—Frankie

Mocha coffincino with extra whipped scream <3 (If I need the caffeine I'll make it a double-shot.)
—Draculaura

Chai latte...plus a death-by-chocolate cupquake or two. Gotta love that employee discount. ;)
—Clawdeen

Someone needs to make you ghouls try a catnipucino—they're whisker-licking good.
—Toralei

Salted Acaramel frappé, with one pump each of rasp-acary and vanilla syrup. My royally secret treat. —Cleo

No one mentioned any of the secret menu items! Am I the only one who knows about the spookies-and-cream iced latte? ;) —Invisi Billy

A scaryberry smoothie with a seaweed-stuffed clawssant...ghoulicious! —Lagoona

No surprise that we both like the hidden menu best...although my favorite is the apple spider frappé. —Twyla

They serve simply marvellous ginger tea as well! Iced or hot, it is equally delightful. —Robecca

Hot deadly nightshade tea and two screampuffs. Sugar fuels brain activity. —Ghoulia

I found photo from Coffin Bean fearleading fundraiser! You ghouls raised much money to go to Monster Mashional competition. Say yak cheese! —Abbey

The time I got totally freaked about being the only ghoul in my group without a boyfiend, and decided to make my own in my dad's lab at home. At least Hoodude has finally forgiven me for creating him and then immediately dumping him before I realized he was actually alive. Not my beast moment.

—Frankie

I'm glad you brought me to unlife, Frankie! Better to have loved and lost, right? Besides, I'm happy to be alive and at Monster High—how else would I have met my bluddies on the graveball team?

—Hoodude

I'm really dead-icated to my vegetarian diet, so any time I see buh...bluh...the b-word, I faint dead away! It's mortalfying every time—but especially when I'm, say, at the top of a fearleading pyramid, or in the middle of a crowded creepateria. I'm so glad I have my ghouls to watch my back!

—Draculaura

The day I forgot to study for a big test because I was too busy watching the final of America's Next Top Monster. The next day I was so panicked that I tried to cheat off of Ghoulia's test—baaad idea. She knew what I was up to and taught me a painful lesson about skullastic honesty. Test failed, but message received.

—Clawdeen

Honesty IS the beast policy. But I am always happy to help you study!

—Ghoulia

The day after I broke up with Clawd was probably the worst day of my unlife. We were only dating because it seemed expected—we were more friends than anything else and the breakup was mutual. I asked Clawd to go along with the story that I'd dumped him, and he did, but that made the whole school turn against me, especially when it came out that I was dating Deuce. It caused monster drama for months. —Cleo

On one of my first days at Monster High, I used a word which in the down under is perfectly normal but up here in the dry world is way, way offensive. I'm not gonna write it down here, it's that bad. Needless to say, I got in really hot water with Headmistress Bloodgood—my dad had to come in and explain the situation. I'm lucky I didn't get expelled!
—Lagoona

sorry about that, ghoul. I'm glad it got cleared up... even if it took awhile.
—Clawdeen

Reading this page made me laugh out loud. How do you ghouls tie your own shoes without werecat levels of luck?
—Toralei

I was school shopping and a callous shoe store lurk tried to close the door in my face, even though there were still a few minutes before closing time. She either didn't understand Zombie or was pretending not to. I was tired and near tears from frustration, but Clawdeen came out of nowhere and saved the day by being her incredibly alpha self. I will never forget her kindness.
—Ghoulia

Anytime, ghoulfriend! —Clawdeen

NAME: Frankie

WORST HABIT: Not being able to pull myself together in a crisis. I've gotten better at it over time, but sometimes I still go to pieces at the worst moments.

NAME: Draculaura

WORST HABIT: I can be a pretty emotional ghoul. You'd think at 1600 I'd have stopped crying over every little thing, but I guess it's just how I am. I wouldn't mind except it does make monsters—especially my dad—treat me like I'm still a little ghoul.

NAME: Ghoulia

WORST HABIT: Letting myself fade into the background. It is an easy trap for us zombies to fall into—we slowly shuffle along, and to an uneducated eye seem to be devoid of personality and individuality. Part of the crowd. I long to overcome this shyness and let my freaky-fabulous flag fly.

NAME: Cleo

WORST HABIT: Letting my sister Nefera get under my bandages. I like to think of myself as a fairly calm and collected ghoul, but Nefera always knows exactly how to make me lose my cool. Someday I hope I can stop caring about what she thinks and just be happy being my dynastic self.

NAME: Lagoona

WORST HABIT: Sometimes I go with the flow a little too much. I don't really like conflict and I'm always trying not to make waves—but there are times when a ghoul has to stand up for herself. Thanks to my friends, I'm learning when those times are.

HANG FIN!

NAME: Clawdeen

WORST HABIT: Bossiness. It's part of being in a big pack at home—you have to claw your way to the top if you want to be an alpha, and sometimes that means stepping on a few paws. It comes in handy sometimes, but I catch myself barking at my friends sometimes, and that's no good.

I know how you feel...when I see a monster littering, or doing something else careless to the environment, I want to step in right away! Having to hold myself back from using my pollens of persuasion can be a fearious struggle sometimes.
—Venus

LET'S GET PERSONAL, GHOULFRIEND

NAME: Frankie

IF I HAVE TO, I'LL SAY:

I'm really flexible in a tight spot, and I always try to look on the bright side of things! I find cheerfulness and optimism can get you through almost anything, no matter how dire the situation seems. Finding the silver lining to even the worst situations is pretty easy for me.

NAME: Draculaura

IF I HAVE TO, I'LL SAY

The same soft heart that makes me wail like a banshee at the drop of a hat is also big enough to care about every creature, big and small. I ♥ all my ghoulfriends so much, and I'll drop everything to help them when they need me.

Ghouls GHOULS GHOULS

NAME: Clawdeen

IF I HAVE TO, I'LL SAY:

I'm monstrously loyal. It doesn't matter what the situation is, I've always got my beasties' backs. I'd drink wolfsbane from a silver chalice no matter how much pain it caused me and ask for more if it'd help them—no questions asked!

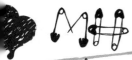

NAME: Cleo

IF I HAVE TO, I'LL SAY:

My royal blood makes me a natural leader. I'm ready and willing to take charge in any situation and turn it around. An unlifetime of bossing around a small army of servants has given me plenty of experience with command.

NAME: Lagoona

IF I HAVE TO, I'LL SAY:

Monsters tell me I'm a fintastic listener. Sometimes all someone needs is a shoulder to cry on and a sympathetic ear, and I'm always there for any of my mates who need me. I might not know how to fix it, but I can at least be there for them when they need me.

NAME: Ghoulia

IF I HAVE TO, I'LL SAY:

My brains are my greatest asset—I may not be fast or athletic, but I am smart, and I am glad to put my intelligence to work in service of my friends and monsterkind. If you need careful planning or a clever scheme, I am your ghoul.

MONSTER High

NAME: Frankie

I'll call up one of my beasties just to chat—
a few minutes of good ghoul talk with a friend
charges me faster than a 9-volt to the bolts!

NAME: Lagoona

It's said that the best way to cheer yourself up
is to cheer someone else up. If I'm feeling blue, I'll
find someone else who's feeling down and dead-icate
myself to making their day better. Even if I can only
improve it a little, being helpful is a great way to
feel better myself.

NAME: Clawdeen

If I'm in a boo funk, I tackle it head-on. I put on my favorite
outfit of the moment, style my hair in the wildest style I
can stand, lock my door, and blast a song by Casta Fierce or
Catty Noir—something a wolf can howl along to.
Usually by the time I've reached the end of the
album, my bad mood is a bad memory.

I'm mighty envious of you! Sure, I'd love to
be able to sing out loud, but I fear most
monsters would run for cover if I opened
my mouth. —Scarah

Consider this an open invitation to come sing
scary-oke with us next time, ghoul. ;) We won't
turn tail and run, promise! —Clawdeen

NAME: Cleo

I go shopping and buy something absolutely ridiculous,
like a pair of gaudy earrings or a belt covered in tiny
bedazzled crocodiles. Then I give it to the next friend
I see. The look of bewilderment on their faces always
cheers me right up.

NAME: Draculaura

I take a nice, long, relaxing
bath, and then lie in my coffin
and read a good book, or paint
my toenails, or cuddle with
Count Fabulous. If you're
stressed or sad, it's nice to
set some time aside to do
nothing at all, no pressure.

NAME: Ghoulia

I download new music or listen to a Podcasket on my
iCoffin. (I am especially fond of "This Zombie Unlife" by
Irot Glass.) I find that listening to something interesting and
new will inspire me to feel better.

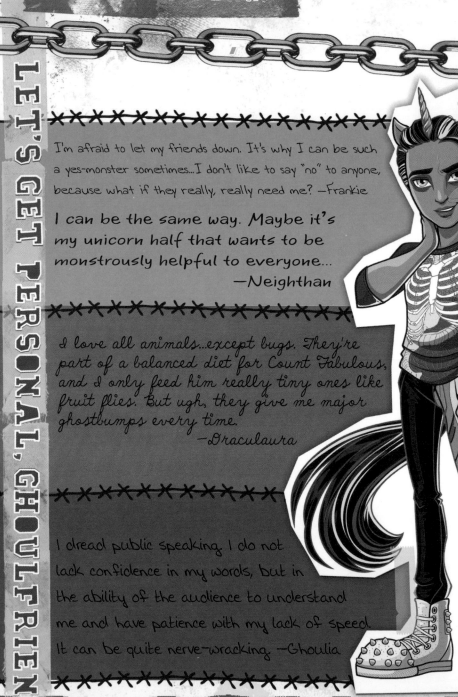

LET'S GET PERSONAL, GHOULFRIEND

I'm afraid to let my friends down. It's why I can be such a yes-monster sometimes...I don't like to say "no" to anyone, because what if they really, really need me? —Frankie

I can be the same way. Maybe it's my unicorn half that wants to be monstrously helpful to everyone... —Neighthan

I love all animals...except bugs. They're part of a balanced diet for Count Fabulous, and I only feed him really tiny ones like fruit flies. But ugh, they give me major ghostbumps every time. —Draculaura

I dread public speaking. I do not lack confidence in my words, but in the ability of the audience to understand me and have patience with my lack of speed. It can be quite nerve-wracking. —Ghoulia

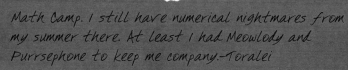

Math Camp. I still have numerical nightmares from my summer there. At least I had Meowlody and Purrsephone to keep me company.—Toralei

The dark. I dare any monster to be sealed in a tomb for a thousand years with nothing but a candle for illumination and see how much they like it. —Cleo

Lightning is a big fear of mine. For a sea monster, getting stuck in a storm at the surface can be monstrously frightening—especially since electricity travels so far in the water. Being friends with Frankie has kind of helped me get over it, though.
—Lagoona

Failure. My fashion-designing dreams are really important to me, and if I can't make them come true...yeah, that even scares this wolf. But I know I've got the skills and talent to pull it off—the only thing that can hold me back is me! —Clawdeen

i too feel this way often. it is good to know i am not alone, amighoul. :) —Skelita

LET'S GET PERSONAL, GHOULFRIEND

ALL ABOUT: Frankie

1. The scary-sweetest ghoul in school!
2. Always has something positive to say.
3. The most genuine monster I've ever met!
4. Never gives up, no matter how much you wish she would.
5. Kind to a fault.

ALL ABOUT: Draculaura

1. Picks you up when you feel down!
2. Would give you the shirt off of her back—and a pair of matching pumps, too.
3. Has the biggest heart of any monster.
4. Forgives and forgets easily.
5. She's the first to step up when you need help.

ALL ABOUT: Clawdeen

1. Loyal and mega-kind, no matter what!
2. Self-confidence to spare!
3. So protective of her friends!
4. I sometimes envy her fierce fashion sense.
5. Never backs down from an injustice.

ALL ABOUT: Cleo

1. Knows how to keep us ghouls working together!
2. Never lets anything hold her back!
3. Throws the beast parties.
4. Doesn't want you to know how scary-sweet she secretly is. ;)
5. Steadfast, trustworthy, and a true ghoulfriend to the end.

ALL ABOUT: Lagoona

1. Easiest ghoul to get along with.
2. Always there when you need her.
3. Beast listener...and beast swimmer, too.
4. Keeps an open mind about everyone.
5. Her capacity for empathy seems limitless.

ALL ABOUT: Ghoulia

1. The ghoul we all rely on!
2. Always has a plan...or three!
3. Smartest ghoul in school. Maybe even the monsterverse. :)
4. Willing to help everyone she meets, no matter what!
5. I know I can trust her with all my heart.

LET'S GET PERSONAL GHOULFRIEND

Didn't you like Jackson? Or was it Holt? Or was it both?? ;)

Oh my ghoul, don't make me answer! I will totally un-die of embarrassment! —Frankie

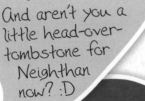

Don't forget your summer crush on Andy Beast :3

I remember a certain new ghoul at school having a major crush on my darling Deuce ;P

And aren't you a little head-over-tombstone for Neighthan now? :D

This is it, guys, I'm un-dying. This is why you don't ask, because one day some monster will say, "Whatever happened to Frankie," and you'll have to say, "It's our fault, we killed her. She un-died of embarrassment."

Slo mo is the sweetest Zombie a ghoul could ask for. We share a lot of common intellectual pursuits, and there is nothing nicer than sittin down with him to talk about mathematical theorems, or just go for a whirl on my scoot I know he sometimes thinks he is not intelligent enough for me, but that is simply untrue—I cherish our differences as much as our similarities. —Ghoulia

My relationship with Deuce is rock-solid, of course. Ever since we started dating, we've been THE power couple of Monster High. Of course, anyone I date is guaranteed to be popular, but Deuce and I go together like hieroglyphics in a cartouche.
—Cleo

Gil and I may have had our high and low tides, but we're still going strong. Through the harshest waves, our relationship has never really floundered, and that gives me a lot of hope that we'll still be together when we're salty old-timers. :)
—Lagoon

It's no secret that Clawd is my romantic wonder-wolf. <3 For a little while I was afraid that the bad feelings between vampires and werewolves would tear us apart, but we've stayed strong! Who's the cutest wolfy at Monster High? He is, yes he is!
—Draculaura

No one at Monster High has been manster enough for me yet, but that's okay. My standards are pretty high, and I'm as patient as the grave when it comes to sniffing out what I want.
—Clawdeen

JUST FOR FUN:
CUTEST THING YOUR PET DOES

Watzit is the cutest when he chases his tail. I mean literally—it falls off sometimes and he can spend hours knocking it around and carrying it in his mouth. At least he's patient while I sew it back on. I guess they do say pets come to resemble their owners... —Frankie

No bat is as fashionable as Count Fabulous! I made him his own online account and post pictures of him in his newest, most adorable outfits, because he just loves to pose. He's the most elegant insectivore in the world!
—Draculaura

Crescent is one fiercely independent feline, and she won't perform on command. Still, when I toss a ball of yarn her way, her eyes get as big as a full moon and she'll roll all over the room like the little predator she is. —Clawdeen

Crescent says her favorite toys are the catnip mice...and she'd like you to bring home more of those as soon as possible. ;)
—Jane

I don't know why so many monsters think snakes are cold and unfeeling—Hissette is just the sweetest. She coils up next to me in my sarcophagus, and if my alarm clock fails to wake me, she tickles my cheek with her tongue until I wake up. —Cleo

It's the same with Rhuen! Monsters think ferrets are weaselly and untrustworthy, but she's so spirited, and has so much love to give!
                    —Spectra

Neptuna is one bright beastie. She knows more than a dozen tricks, from "play dead" to "triple backflip." But my favorite is the fishy kisses she gives when she's really excited to see me. <3
                    —Lagoona

I have been trying to teach Sir Hoots-a-Lot to carry my mail, like in a certain book series I enjoy. But so far all he does is shred the envelopes with his beak. He likes to roll around in the bits of paper until they stick to his feathers like snow—I have to admit, it is dreadfully darling.
                    —Ghoulia

JUST FOR FUN:

LIST THREE THINGS
YOU CAN'T UNLIVE WITHOUT

NAME: Frankie

1. Electricity, obvs. ;)
2. A sewing kit, too...
3. and my die-ary

NAME: Clawdeen

1. My sketchbook
2. My iCoffin loaded with my favorite tunes
3. My favorite pair of Alexander McScream heels

NAME: Draculaura

1. A notebook for poetry and story ideas
2. At least one cute accessory
3. Fresh fruits and veggies!

NAME: Cleo

If I had to only choose three things to live with, I would rather un-die....Okay, okay.

1. My iCoffin
2. My dear Hissette
3. A fright-light

NAME: Lagoona

1. Monsturizer
2. Clean water
3. Some decent surf is all this ghoul needs. :)

NAME: Ghoulia

1. My glasses
2. My ever-present laptop
3. An umbrella—I can't exactly run from the rain

NAME: Frankie

FASHION TIP: I dig bold patterns—try mixing and matching for some fangtastic looks that are ferociously fashion-forward!

NAME: Draculaura

FASHION TIP: Don't neglect the little details. The right pair of shoes, the perfect pair of earrings, the ideal necklace—these can make or break your lurk!

NAME: Clawdeen

FASHION TIP: Go fierce without fear! No one ever made fashion history by being conservative and doing what other monsters have already done, so change it up. Layer creatively, clash colors, wear socks over tights under shorts! Be your confident, freaky-fabulous self and the pack will follow.

NAME: Cleo
FASHION TIP: I understand that not everyone can afford to shop like a deNile, so a good strategy is to invest in pieces with immortal appeal and build your outfits around them. I have pieces that have lasted for a thousand years, and they're still cutting-edge.

NAME: Lagoona
FASHION TIP: Dress for comfort as well as appearance. Your clothes could be the trendiest ever, but if they're too itchy or tight or awkward to wear, then what's the point? A ghoul shouldn't have to suffer for style.

Stripes are always in!
—Toralei

NAME: Ghoulia
FASHION TIP:

Don't be hesitant about turning to your ghoulfriends for assistance. If I am unsure if an outfit "works," I will take a photo on my iCoffin and send it to Cleo for critique, because I trust her sense of style.

JUST FOR FUN:

WHO'S THE LAST MONSTER

YOU TEXTED AND WHY?

NAME: Frankie

WHO I TEXTED:

Neighthan Rot. I was just asking him about our Bite-ology homework, though! I swear!

NAME: Draculaura

WHO I TEXTED:

Iris Clops. I totes required her advice about some constellations I was referencing in my latest short story. That ghou knows stargazing!

It was my pleasure, Draculaura! I'm always happy to share my passion with a new ghoulfriend. :)
—Iris

NAME: Clawdeen

WHO I TEXTED: My big sis Clawdia. I was sending her beast wishes from the family while she studies scream writing abroad. I miss her terribly as our pack is as close as they come. I don't think she minds being a lone werewolf of Londoom, though ;)

NAME: Cleo

WHO I TEXTED: Deuce, to triple-check our plans for our date this weekend. I have to be sure he didn't forget to make reservations at the new monsterlecular gastronomy restaurant he wanted to take me to.

LIKE I'D FORGET! I'VE BEEN COILED UP WITH EXCITEMENT SINCE YOU SUGGESTED IT.

—DEUCE

NAME: Lagoona

WHO I TEXTED: I texted Abbey to wish her good luck in her snowboarding competition this weekend. I know she's going to tear up the snow like a beast!

NAME: Ghoulia

WHO I TEXTED: Gilda Goldstag—she is the treasurer of the student disembodied council, and I wanted to make sure she received my budget proposal for the Monster High chess club.

Am looking forward to it. Especially since fearleading squad with ghoulfriends will be there to cheer for me.   —Abbey

NAME: Frankie

ACCESSORY: My electrifying plush purse! Clawdeen helped me pick it out before I started at Monster High, and it has remained my fave ever sinc

NAME: Draculaura

ACCESSORY: Ok my ghoul, there is no way I can choose just one of my fangtastic accessories as my favorite! Um, I suppose my extra thick sunbrella, because I might get frightfully burned without it.

NAME: Clawdeen

ACCESSORY: A fierce pair of shoes. Don't ask me which ones—you might as well ask my mom to pick her favorite cub. They're all my favorites, and that's my final word. ;P

Oh my Rah!

NAME: Cleo

ACCESSORY: My bandages. I can't be seen without my burial wrappings...literally, I would crumble to dust without them. Fortunately, I am able to style them as I see fit, so they always match what I'm wearing.

NAME: Lagoona

ACCESSORY: My fishbowl purse—I have to take Neptuna with me wherever I go, or she can get lonely and snappish. I'd never want to leave her behind, anyway!

NAME: Ghoulia

ACCESSORY: My spooktacular spectacles are my must-have. Not being able to see your hand in front of your face is definitely a fashion faux-pas.

Freaky fab final words:

You ghouls are the beast! I had so much fun learning even more about you! —Frankie

---

Reading all these responses made me want to cry like a little ghoul. You are all so scary sweet and I love you all to undeath!
—Draculaura

You ghouls make me proud to be your friend!
—Clawdeen

To all my mates: You are my finspiration! <3
I couldn't imagine unlife without you :)
—Lagoona

It's nice to know we all struggle with freaky flaws sometimes....
Even me.
—Cleo

I am honored to count such wonderful ghouls among my friends. —Ghoulia

ROCK YOUR RIGHT TO
♥ ♥ ♥ ♥ FRIGHT